two cats sitting
at a window

Other novels by the author published by
Hannacroix Creek Books, Inc.

I See Yellow Flowers in the Green Grass

Nguyen Nhat Anh

translation by Nha Thuyen and Kaitlin Rees illustration by
Do Hoang Tuong

Two Cats Sitting at a Window

a fable

From the beloved and bestselling
original in Vietnamese, *Có hai con mèo ngồi bên cửa sổ*

Hannacroix Creek Books, Inc.
Stamford, Connecticut

Published by Hannacroix Creek Books, Inc.
in English except in Vietnam in October
2025

Hannacroix Creek Books, Inc.
1127 High Ridge Road, #110
Stamford, CT 06905 USA
https://www.hcbooks.us
e-mail: hannacroix@aol.com

For translation rights inquiries, use the
Contact Us page at https://www.hcbooks.us

Cover design by Andres Alvez

Interior illustrations by Do Hoang Tuong

The English language edition, translated by
Nha Thuyen and Kaitlin Rees, and the
illustrations by Do Hoang Tuong, originally
published by Tre Publishing Company in
Vietnam, are reused with their permission.

Two Cats Sitting at a Window is a work of fiction.
Any resemblance to actual events, locales, or
persons, living or dead, is entirely coincidental.

ISBN: 978-1-938998-19-5 (trade paperback)

Two cats sitting at a window
One stays the other goes

N. N. A.

*T*his morning, like every morning for the past two weeks, around 9 am, as the morning chill is letting up and the neighbor's frangipani tree stops shaking off its leaves, Queen Last Year pokes her head out the window to watch her cat and let out her habitual sigh.

Bear Cat lies there, on the balcony, delightedly embracing every ray of early sunshine. With his body leaning into a shadow, back glued to the floral-print tiles, four legs leisurely splayed, eyes half-closed, he lazily enjoys life.

The type of person (or cat) who sprawls out in such an extremely self-satisfied way would certainly inspire annoyance in others, if not jealousy.

Queen Last Year watches Bear Cat with a look full of criticism, but she doesn't speak a word. She simply releases a gentle shrug, then goes back to her kitchen to get busy with a mound of dough that's been whitening her hands since morning.

Should you be as keenly observant as the author, you might also notice the appearance of a slight frown that accompanies the gentle shrug of Queen Last Year. This would be on account of the fact that Bear Cat, whom Princess Ivy brought home two weeks ago, has proven himself to be the most useless on earth. Not only because he has not caught a single mouse in the last three hundred and thirty-six interminable hours (despite there being squeaking mice day and night), but also for the way he so languidly bathes there in the sun making it plainly obvious that no one should have any expectations of him in the slightest. All of this increasingly disheartens the Queen.

2

*O*f course, Bear Cat knows well that Queen Last Year is upset with him. He's an intelligent cat.

He also feels grateful to Princess Ivy for rescuing him from the wholesale farm where animals are purchased for slaughter.

And because Princess Ivy is daughter to Queen Last Year, he therefore feels a bit guilty.

But, as sometimes happens in the human species as well, cats have times when they don't want to do the things that someone else wants them to do.

Bear Cat falls into such a situation: he's troubled by being a cat who takes no pleasure in hunting mice, and also troubled by that troubled feeling.

It's not that Bear Cat likes mice—the mischievous rodents give him a nightly headache—but neither

does he like the matter of pouncing upon them just to show off like other cats.

Perhaps stray cats are more keen on catching mice, Bear Cat thinks while raising a paw to swat a fly buzzing before his face. Without proper homes, street cats have to fend for themselves for food, sifting through dumps or prowling around marketplaces. If they are going to be thieves, they must be brilliantly gifted! The owner of a fish stall just looks away for a moment and those cats can nab a fish faster than lightning. So of course, when hunting a mouse, they don't miss a single chance out of a hundred.

Then again, the majority of cats like to catch mice just for fun, a way to waste their spare time. No real need for food. Most cats enjoy fish the best. And, as far as house cats are concerned, mouse meat is quite unappetizing—something only for those undiscriminating stray cats.

*B*ear Cat used to live under the same roof with a calico mademoiselle. Ah, memories. He had given her the name Floral Top, following the fashion of those contemporary gents who fondly call their ladies names like Babe, or My Sad Tiny Pebble.

Floral Top was a truly noble and elegant cat. She would stroll around with a great deal of grace. Cats, as you must know, especially the female ones, always seem to walk like noble ladies. She even looked elegant in her sleep. Floral Top never slept in dirty or damp places.

Mornings, she used to amble leisurely toward the front yard and then exquisitely lay down to sunbathe. Evenings, she would saunter slowly back to the attic where she'd then cuddle into the comforts of her handmade bed, something her mistress had assembled from pieces of wood and covered with pillows and cushions.

On the topic of sleep, Bear Cat's favorite spot used to be an old bookcase, where he'd like to curl himself up between books on the wide shelf. On his right, were some dictionaries enveloped in a scattering of dust. On his left, stood a porcelain plate with sailboats drawn at the bottom. Next to that, a rubber doll with messy hair who always looked a bit jealous of his own silky smooth fur.

Before Bear Cat was kidnapped by cat burglars and sold to the wholesale farm, he used to invite Floral Top to sunbathe with him on the balcony where he would rub up against her so they'd look like a pair of cotton balls leaning into one another, and with half-closed eyes he'd wait for her to paw gently at his back. Patting just for the sake of patting, without any concrete purpose. But such a caress would be more than enough to take Bear Cat over the moon.

On rainy days, he'd ask her to climb up on the windowsill to sit and admire the rain before having to happily snuggle up from the chill, using any excuse for a chance to be close to each other.

In those days, he became quite the poet.

Floral Top inspired in Bear Cat dozens of poems, each one as soft as silk and as potent as wine. To be fair, one might say, his poems are no less interesting than those of the author's.

*H*ere is Bear Cat's first poem for Floral Top:

> *Purr purr purr... Meow...*
> *Meow meow meow...*
> *Purr purr purr...*
> *Meow meow... purr purr...*
> *Purr purr... meow meow...*

Whenever reciting a poem to Floral Top, Bear Cat would feel a hidden engine revving a gentle and steady sound from somewhere in his soft fur. It's a sound that, in the realm of cat senses, is more melodious than any other music on earth.

Apparently, however, the author needs to translate the poem so you too, dear readers, can enjoy and admire Bear Cat's gift for poetry.

Here is our human language translation:

Has my baby love gone to bed
I have just rested my loving head
A lovely candle gives its lovely glow
Through this loving heart my love does flow...

Oh, how many times "love" appears in a poem of just four lines! Perhaps because of this repeated word, the poem touches Floral Top's heart so deeply that she pats a paw across Bear poet's back, an act reserved for feelings of the most incredible satisfaction.

5

But now, since being separated from Floral Top, Bear Cat feels his life has become lifeless. If Princess Ivy didn't rescue him from that wholesaler, perhaps he wouldn't even fear death.

> *Whispering adieu, brief at night*
> *By the doorstep the rain flies*

The days he spent locked behind iron bars, he thought of Floral Top much more often than of death. One night, he sang these two sentimental lines while leaning back on the cage's iron walls, watching the rain fall into thick grass, feeling his nostalgic soul grow moss.

(Henceforth, for your convenience, dear readers, the author will provide human-language translations without citing the animal-language original, as the author doesn't need to prove himself as a polyglot anyway!)

Unaware of his hidden love, Queen Last Year gets irritated with Bear Cat.

But how could a lovesick cat possibly be motivated to hunt for mice? Not to mention that even before having to part with Floral Top, he was never the kind of cat who could be bothered to move a paw in the direction of a mouse.

Ah, there was that one time though. The only time Bear Cat belligerently jumped upon a little house mouse. He had been in the middle of a dreamy recitation of poetry to Floral Top, and right at the most lyrical line, *"Here dear Floral Top..."* a squeak from under the cupboard demolished the romantic air that he had been so carefully constructing with the budding verses in his head.

In a fit of rage, he pounced down and whacked the little grinch in one fell swoop.

Easy as pie.

He wanted to rebuke the little mouse, but the poor thing had already fainted from fright.

Bear Cat had just dropped the timid creature to the floor and began strolling over to Floral Top when Susu, the puppy of the house, bounded over and picked the mouse right up.

The puppy pranced all around the house showing off his talent with the little mouse draped across his muzzle. Like a hero on a victory lap, he purposefully passed by the desk where his mistress was studying.

Believing the little mouse to be dead already, he never would've guessed that his leaping about would bring the little creature back to consciousness. Squeak! Hearing an unexpected sound from his own mouth (but clearly not his own sound), the panic-stricken Susu immediately spit out the mouse and fled with his tail between his legs.

Thus was the second accidental impression that Bear Cat made in young Floral Top's heart: bringing her a peal of laughter on a morning filled with the wonderful mix of lyrical poetry and lighthearted comedy—joys that are not always available to cats (or humans).

Bear Cat closes his eyes to calm his soul. He is of the belief that he can listen to his emotions much more thoroughly when his mind is not distracted by the visual. And it was true—that whole morning, his heart had been so bright imagining himself with Floral Top, lying by her side under a rainbow's arch. He had hoped that life would pass this way forever, under the beautiful shadow of fortune's umbrella.

Fantasizing such a scene, Bear Cat never would have guessed that that morning would be the last in which he could bathe himself in the sweet fragrance of happiness. Were he to be as experienced as the author of this book, he would understand that excessive happiness can sometimes be nothing but a trap.

6

*O*verall, since Bear Cat first set paws in the palace, neither the sound of running mice nor their squeaking about has subsided in the least. Queen Last Year sullenly concludes that Princess Ivy's campaign to liberate Bear Cat from the wholesalers on Reed Road was a complete and utter failure. Bear Cat shows no inclination to prove his worth is greater than the inanimate iron bars of the traps that King Next Year brought home.

Queen Last Year lets out a sigh, looking melancholy and lost.

"*Last year* our old Tabby was so much more eager to hunt mice than this Bear Cat! Tabby was a stray, but truly excellent."

Princess Ivy tries defending Bear Cat, but even she

hears how feeble her argument sounds. "But Tabby was a wild cat, Mom."

King Next Year runs his ten fingers through his thick hair, breathing heavily, "*Next year* I will bring Tabby back!"

Surprised, Princess Ivy blinks her long eyelashes in a way that is clearly not a pose. "But can you do that, Dad? You already gave Tabby away!"

"They will accept it." The King resolutely answers, removing his hands from his hair as a sign of confidence. "I'll bring in Bear Cat to trade him for Tabby!"

Queen Last Year shrugs, "Slothful, sluggish, neglectful, idle, good for nothing, head in the clouds— Bear Cat is just like a poet!"

Of course, the Queen doesn't know that Bear Cat truly is a poet.

7

*O*nly Mademoiselle Floral Top knows that secret.

Even Princess Ivy, the guardian of Bear Cat, doesn't know.

The palace mice know even less.

To them, a cat could never be a poet. Cats—the most obnoxious species on earth, the most dangerous, vicious enemy of mice.

Every night, in their deep, damp cave in the earth beneath the palace basement, the mice circle up to hear the lectures of Professor Grande Sewer Rat.

Professor Sewer Rat always starts his lectures with the loud clapping of a ruler against a board while screaming, "Let them die!"

"Let them die, all cats!"

"There's only one cat in this palace!" Little Tom Thumb hesitantly cuts in.

Tom Thumb is the tiniest mouse among the tiny mice. Next to the professor, he's like a fragment of a grain next to a sweet potato. But besides that, Tom Thumb is a spry little mouse.

"Arrogant!" Prof. Grande Rat scowls at Tom Thumb. "I said 'cats,' generally speaking."

Prof. raises the ruler high above his head.

"We must remain determined, even in our sleep! Cats are the thorn in our eyes!"

After a brief pause, Prof. again claps the ruler on the board before raising his voice.

"Better yet, the thorn in our hearts!"

Tom Thumb mumbles, "If we've got a thorn in our heart, it'll be us who will die, not the cats!"

In the quiet of the cave, even Tom Thumb's low voice manages to reach the ears of every mouse. Half of the mice worriedly look at him. The remaining half nervously look up at Prof. Grande.

"Rubbish!" Prof. screams, his thick whiskers quiver. "Lame one, step forward!"

8

*T*om Thumb hobbles to the center of the circle, his tiny tail dragging on the ground as if he were pulling along a string of grey wool.

Tom Thumb is a crippled mouse.

"Who asked you to speak out in class?" Prof. Grande Rat furiously shouts while drumming his ruler on the poor little mouse's head.

It just so happens that the little mouse holds a pencil in his hand at this time. And it's not that he tries to use it against Prof., of course, it's simply a natural reflex when he retracts his neck and both hands rise to cover his head.

The ruler meets Tom Thumb's pencil with a "crack".

Flying from Prof.'s hands, the ruler lands in a corner of the cave.

The whole circle of mice clearly sees Prof.'s trembling fury. They too tremble out of fear and their fondness for Tom Thumb.

"What the hell?" Prof.'s hand, now without a ruler, savagely grabs a piece of Tom Thumb's ear, thin as a budding leaf, and then launches the little one through the air.

Before the wide eyes of terrified mice, Tom Thumb flies over to where Prof.'s ruler has landed. The force of Prof.'s throw, a physical strength that the mice had yet to see until now, was like that of someone determined to cast away every ounce of their anger.

"If you're lucky enough to still be alive, bring the ruler back here!"

Before finding himself swatted through the air like a shuttlecock, Little Tom Thumb could manage to utter only one word: "Mom!"

As you can see, just as we humans often call out for our mothers in times of danger or distress, so too did little Tom Thumb. "Mom"—that loving word often exclaimed when people (and mice) find no one else to cling to. But why include this specific detail? Well, as everyone in the mouse commune knows, Tom Thumb's mother had passed away exactly three months, eight days, twelve hours, and thirty-six minutes before Prof. Grande Sewer Rat mercilessly threw him at the cave's wall.

9

*C*rash!

The whole mice commune close their eyes in unison. Solemnly, dreadfully, mournfully, they believe they are sending the soul of an unfortunate mouse up to heaven.

But then, all eyes open again in unison.

It's unbelievable. Tom Thumb, with a pencil in one hand and the ruler in the other, tentatively crawls forth from the dark cave.

The old mice stroke their whiskers, whispering a thanks to God. The young mice stomp their paws excitedly on the cave floor, only reluctantly stopping when their mothers pinch their ears.

But nothing can hold back the wave of applause that unexpectedly bursts when little Tom Thumb stands before Prof. Grande Sewer Rat looking neither shaky or feeble. That is to say, the excitement of that magical moment surpasses the fear.

Prof. Grande snatches the ruler and bangs the board behind his back.

"Whack!"

Like a bomb hitting the roof of the cave, all mice are instantly dead quiet. The only noise is that of the faint-hearted mice dropping to the floor.

"Good!"

Prof. Grande's voice rings out. At first the mice think it's a word of satisfaction for the miracle of Tom Thumb's victory over death, but his dreadful tone of voice veers from their expectation.

As if to confirm their worry, Prof. Grande points the ruler at the cave's wall, and snaps a cold command.

"Come forward."

*O*n total shock, all eyes immediately follow Prof.'s pointing.

A moment later, the corner of a white ear juts out from darkness.

"Floral Bitty!"

A little mouse gently cries out.

Floral Bitty is a Mademoiselle Guinea Pig. It was Tom Thumb who first met her trembling at the base of a trash bin beside a lamppost one night when he was wandering the streets in search of food (though in search of fun is more accurate).

When Tom Thumb spotted her, Floral Bitty was looking truly devastated. She'd been cold and hungry ever since escaping from a laboratory several days

ago. But in spite of her frail appearance, Tom Thumb believed he'd never seen a rodent more beautiful.

"What are you doing here?"

Tom Thumb had asked her out of curiosity, realizing as he approached that she did in fact resemble a piglet.

"I'm hungry."

"Where is your home?"

"I don't know." Mademoiselle Guinea Pig was hesitant to answer. "It seems I don't have any place to call home."

It was at that moment that Tom Thumb put his hand on the black and white fur of his new friend.

"So lovely you are! Is that a floral dress you're wearing?"

"I'm hungry."

Mademoiselle Guinea Pig's answer in no way fit Tom Thumb's question. Nevertheless, the little mouse took no offense. He nuzzled his new friend's shoulder.

"Follow me then. I will find something for you to eat."

From that day forward, Mademoiselle Guinea Pig stayed with the commune of mice in the palace.

And as a rodent dressed in floral print among a whole nest of mice wearing grey, and being the smallest one to ever live in the palace, and, most importantly, being that Tom Thumb first called her by this name, she became known among the commune as Floral Bitty.

*A*nd so it was that a little white flap of a twitching ear was the first thing the mice saw as Mademoiselle Guinea Pig timidly crept out from the back of the cave.

For Floral Bitty was not an earless guinea pig. It's that she had one white ear and one fully black, and the darker one was completely subsumed into the blackness of the cave.

Now we behold Floral Bitty sheepishly standing before Prof. Grande Sewer Rat. The mice quickly understand it was she who risked catching Tom Thumb before he was smashed like a meatball against the cave's wall.

"Seems you've forgotten your place as a guest here." Prof. Grande suppresses his fury into these contemptuous words.

"I... I..."

Mademoiselle Guinea Pig stammers, not daring to raise her eyes to Prof..

"Looks like I'll either have to put you back out on the streets..."

At this point you can imagine Floral Bitty and Tom Thumb cowering in fear.

"...or think of a good punishment for you."

Prof. Grande's wicked eyes buzz around like two bumblebees deciding where and how to sting, and eventually land on Tom Thumb's face.

"Ah, I nearly forgot about the lame one! So there will be punishments for both of you then!"

Prof. brandishes his ruler but needs to wave it around for some time as he can't think of an appropriate punishment for the two stubborn rodents.

Suddenly his eyes fall on the pencil in Tom Thumb's hand.

"Ah, so our little scamp is an artist!"

Prof. Grande nods while continuing in a sinister voice.

"Then I've got it. You must not be scared of cats since you don't heed my words, right?"

"No sir, I am scared of them..."

Tom Thumb whimpers a panicked reply. Though unsure of where Prof. Grande is going, he feels a trap waiting for him somewhere.

As if not hearing Tom Thumb, or hearing but not registering, Prof. points his ruler in Tom Thumb's face and growls.

"You listen here!"

*T*om Thumb is crazy about drawing.

He draws anywhere it's possible for his pencil to strike: a carton of green beans, a box of cheese, a sleeve of potato chips, an empty can of milk, even a tiny matchbox.

Everyone in the mice commune finds Tom Thumb's drawings quite lovely. He draws flowers, leaves, grains of rice, and drops of rain. He also makes drawings of birds, ants, bees, dragonflies, and of course, mice.

The elders often stand before him, attentive and solemn.

"Draw a majestic portrait of me, son! So that one day after I'm gone..."

"Be sure to make me look stunning, eh!"

"After her, draw this grandma over here!"

Tom Thumb understands the psyche of his "customers". He never fails to draw thick fur for the great grandpa mice who, though sadly hairless, are still delusionally proud of their appearance. And he bestows grace and elegance on all portraits of the madame and mademoiselle mice, giving them a basket of flowers to swing or even a bow to wear.

Tom Thumb's peers urge him to draw comics and then circle around to watch and giggle.

Long story short, if you ever had a chance to see these drawings by Tom Thumb, you would immediately agree that Tom Thumb is a truly talented artist.

While Tom Thumb can draw everything on earth, he has never drawn a cat. Simply because he's never had enough time to carefully observe one. Upon hearing any strange rustling, he has usually already slipped away into the cave.

And now Prof. is demanding that he draw a cat. It wouldn't be a big deal if he could just sketch something from memory, as he is skillful enough to draw a recognizable cat. However, Prof. demands a portrait of a cat who is lying on its back with its four legs pointing up to the sky, looking battered, ugly, and poor. And it should have two mice pulling it by the tail as if it were a wet rag.

Of course, this is all possible. The impossible part is that Prof. Grande Sewer Rat also demands that Tom Thumb and Floral Bitty carry the provocative drawing past Bear Cat as he sunbathes, making no less than three laps around him.

In all their time on earth, never have the mice ever seen such a terrifying punishment.

What's more, Tom Thumb has a limp.

*T*om Thumb's limp comes from exactly one month and fourteen days before, when he got stuck in one of King Next Year's traps. Even the King himself cut his finger when setting the traps, which is why he later transitioned to cats.

But before that, so many mice met their miserable deaths thanks to the omnipresence of traps in the palace.

It was just a lucky chance that Tom Thumb didn't follow the same unfortunate fate of those mice. The trap that got him sprang prematurely, just as he was placing a paw on the metal edge, but before he could get his mouth around the delicious food. "Snap!"

Scared out of his mind, he ran with lifted tail as if being chased by death, unaware that a piece of his hand had been cut.

And because mice use both hands and legs to move, he has been walking with a limp ever since.

And now Prof. Grande Sewer Rat demands the mouse with a limp pull the cat's leg, a game as dangerous as playing with death.

That whole evening and nearly all the next morning, the only thing Tom Thumb can think of is death, as if his head were steeped in mud. He thinks and thinks about it so much that he eventually wonders: could death be thinking about him as well?

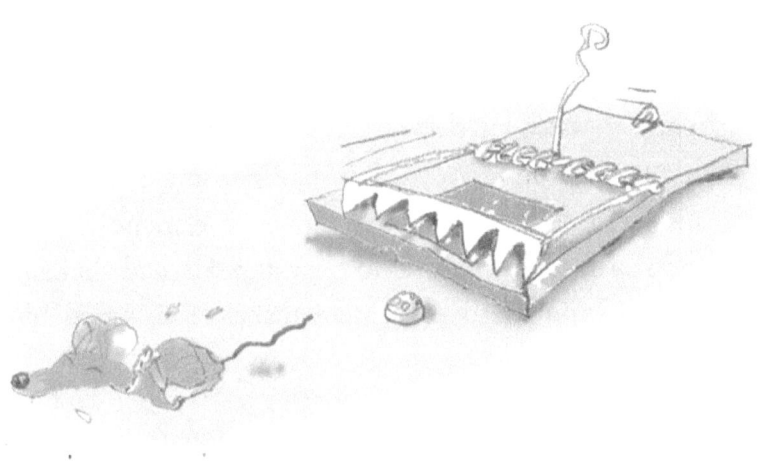

14

This morning, a sunny winter morning, Bear Cat once again stretches out on the balcony, admiring the falling leaves.

Just yesterday it rained the whole day. He recalls how the image of Floral Top had poured into his mind while he was lying there watching the rain.

The drumming of the rain had become a whisper, surrounding him, trapping him in melancholy and transforming his heart into a swamp. He had shaken his head and gently stroked a whisker of his beard, in sorrowful reverie.

> *Your hand waving somewhere far, far away*
> *Could it be that my heart is raining?*

He was envisioning the scene of Floral Top looking up at him with her wet eyes that day he was taken away. Her nose and mouth had been wet as well. Perhaps she had cried. She couldn't do anything for him. She was helpless. But that doesn't make him stop missing her.

His head sank lower and lower in the cold air, as if beaten down by sadness, while his eyes languidly dropped to the patches of black that covered his despondently outstretched arms. For though he was a white cat, Bear Cat's four limbs were black from the toes up to the elbows. Princess Ivy liked to call him a Puss in Socks. But that was yesterday.

two cats sitting at a window

Today the sky began to brighten and by 9 am the sun was shining. The leaves filtering sunbeams through the neighbor's frangipani tree appear more sheer and their green becomes as fresh as rice seedlings.

Meanwhile, the golden leaves quietly depart from their branches with each passing wind.

Bathing himself in that warm sun, Bear Cat senses that he's experiencing the most beautiful moments a winter morning can offer: sun purifying the air, the leaves, and even the sadness that troubles his heart and mind.

He mindlessly counts the leaves falling across his eyes.

> *One leaf falling*
> *Falling now two*
> *Three leaves falling*
> *Falling now four*

It should come as no surprise that Bear Cat, a natural-born poet, counts as if he's making a poem.

> *Three leaves fall against the current*
> *Six tumble down with it...*

The leaves go on dancing through Bear Cat's mind until he spots something he's never once seen before.

*B*ear Cat's jaw drops upon seeing a little house mouse and a guinea pig crawl out from beneath the cupboard.

He rubs his eyes over and over again to make sure he's not dreaming.

What in heaven's name is happening? The shocked Bear Cat watches the two rodents in disbelief. For a mouse to appear in daylight is rare enough, let alone two of them carrying something the way humans carry a banner in a parade.

Taken by surprise, Bear Cat doesn't know how to react. He's nearly motionless as the two creatures scamper past him.

And when the rodents run past him a second time, Bear Cat is still frozen in a state of shock. As he gently inches forward with cotton-soft steps, he is still not sure what to do. Bewildered, he anxiously explores his emotions and considers his moves.

He suspects the two rodents are playing some game. But what the game is he can't figure out. And how on earth can rodents dare to play in front of a cat? He turns these questions around in his mind with no answer. He only feels that it's a serious blow to his pride. Finally, he decides what he should do.

Creeping forward to what he thinks is an appropriate distance, Bear Cat crouches down and shifts his weight to his hind legs, preparing to pounce.

16

When the rodents provoke him for a third time by crossing before his eyes, still clutching some paper in their mouths, Bear Cat is no longer surprised. All his thoughts are now totally focused on pouncing.

In the blink of an eye, Bear Cat is suddenly flying through the air like a white ball hurled from some secret launch pad. And then, fast as lightning, he lengthens himself just enough to land precisely on his target.

His arms stretch and his claws extend like pincers.

Bear Cat executes his pounce in such a perfect and graceful way that other wild cats would surely be jealous.

But while he is so sure that he's caught the rodents and is holding one in each hand (for even the author is quite sure of it as well), the reality is that he's only caught the empty air.

An astute reader could certainly deduce the cause of his failure: when undertaking this hazardous task, Tom Thumb and Floral Bitty naturally were staying on high alert. They clearly knew where Bear Cat was lying and that he could pounce at any moment.

Rather than waiting for Bear Cat to land, the pair dropped the paper and hightailed it out of there upon detecting the first slight change of wind.

*B*ut almost immediately, Bear Cat instinctively performs a second pounce without a moment's thought to why his previous attempt failed. His feet move light years ahead of his thoughts and feelings.

This time, it's only Mademoiselle Guinea Pig who can escape.

The poor little mouse scurries over to the wooden cupboard, but before he can slip beneath it, he feels something like cold metal squeezing the back of his neck and nailing him to the floor.

Without realizing what's happening, his body is pulled up through the air.

His mind drifts away as if in a dream and suddenly Tom Thumb's head is completely empty. He only can recall one name, which he cries out as both a plea for help and as a painful moan.

"Floral Bitty!"

Bear Cat scoops the little mouse up as easily as a little toy, almost weightless.

But the mouse's panicked cry startles the cat.

He takes a few steps back and sets Tom Thumb on the ground, still holding him in his paws. With a hoarse voice, he questions the little one.

"What did you just say?"

His ears still whirring, Tom Thumb doesn't hear Bear Cat. But he again instinctively cries out in despair.

"Floral Bitty!"

It's a cry that happens to save his life.

*B*ear Cat suddenly remembers his Mademoiselle Floral Top. From the moment Tom Thumb first cried out Floral Bitty's name, he felt as if someone punched him in the chest.

Bear Cat was about to ask who Floral Bitty was, but realized he didn't need to. He had seen the guinea pig. He understood why she was called Floral Bitty. He had similarly called his calico Mademoiselle Floral Top for her coat of many colors.

As Tom Thumb's consciousness gradually returns, he is astonished to realize that he's still alive.

He cautiously looks up to Bear Cat and, for the first time in his life, is able to hold his gaze upon a cat at such a close distance.

Initially he feels a bit scared, remembering Prof.

Grande Sewer Rat's lecture on how sinister and evil cats are. However, a kind of peaceful calm gradually enters his body and curiosity soon replaces the fear in his heart.

He senses that Bear Cat is not all that interested in him. Bear Cat's eyes are cast off into the distant sky and though his claws continue to clutch Tom Thumb's neck, they have greatly relaxed.

This cat doesn't seem the least bit predatory! A contemplative cat, perhaps even melancholy! With this in mind, Tom Thumb tries to escape the claws by wiggling his tiny head a bit.

Bear Cat looks down at the little mouse and shakes his head.

"Nowhere for you to run, little one!"

He then releases a sigh.

"Floral Bitty is your girlfriend?"

"Girlfriend?"

Tom Thumb doesn't get it; he's never heard the word "girlfriend" before. He widens his tiny eyes, still no bigger than a grain of rice, and appears to sink deep in thought.

Bear Cat realizes that Tom Thumb is still naive to such matters.

"It's okay if you can't answer that!" He sighs again. "But, do you like Floral Bitty?"

"Yes, of course! I like her very much!"

Tom Thumb answers immediately, more hastily than necessary. For it's true, he likes her very much.

Bear Cat asks another question somewhat aimlessly, his voice softening.

"And have you ever had to part with her?"

"So far, no. Not yet."

"How happy you must be!"

Tom Thumb is familiar with the word "happy". He once overheard a discussion among the elder mice on this subject. But a cat congratulating a mouse on being happy is something he's never heard before.

Tom Thumb senses that it's not quite relevant to discuss happiness in this particular situation, but the words blurted out of this cat's mouth are like a sudden shower of delight pouring onto his heart.

19

$\mathcal{B}$ear Cat had congratulated the little mouse's happiness, however his voice was tinged with sadness. He wanted to ask more questions, but realized the conversation would just be the melancholy echoes of his troubled soul.

Deciding to dig no further into his innermost feelings, Bear Cat turns his head to see the paper on the floor. Only now does he recognize that it's a drawing.

With one hand still holding Tom Thumb, he pulls the drawing closer with the other.

And upon seeing the details of the drawing, he feels puzzled.

"You drew this, eh?" Bear Cat's voice sharpens and his eyes narrow at the little mouse, feeling angered but also somewhat amused.

"Yes." Tom Thumb's voice is barely audible while his tiny heart pounds in his chest.

Bear Cat turns back to the drawing. The strokes create a dynamic and comical portrait of a cat who really does resemble Bear Cat, his white fur and black legs being dragged along by the mice.

"So are you just bored of living, little one?"

Though Bear Cat's question could appear threatening, his tone of voice remains as calm as if he were talking about weather.

Tom Thumb can recognize the cat's calm demeanor but still feels unsettled, as if Bear Cat's question rakes his heart.

"No... Not me..." Tom Thumb hears his frantic plea and immediately realizes the contradiction in his reply. Clumsily, he adds, "Right, well it was me... But I did it only because I got punished."

Tom Thumb then tells Bear Cat about Professor Grande Sewer Rat.

"Such a sinister old rat! Clearly he just wanted to push you into a death trap!" Bear Cat retracts his claws while commenting on the poor little mouse's breathless story.

This unexpected act leaves Tom Thumb in such disbelief that he doesn't even try to flee. He instead reflects on how Bear Cat is actually far less intimidating than Prof..

"So you think Prof. wanted me to die?" The question causes Tom Thumb some pain, for he already knows the answer. He's been answering that question to himself since yesterday.

"What else could it be? He knows well that you can't run fast!"

Bear Cat looks down at the little mouse, his voice suddenly growing distant.

"But if you were to die, imagine how sad little Floral Bitty would be!"

*T*om Thumb doesn't understand why the cat appears so interested in the friendship between him and Floral Bitty. This is the second time that Bear Cat brings it up. He seems to be pondering much more about happiness and sorrow rather than... mouse meat! As Tom Thumb considers this peculiarity, the seed of affection sprouts in his heart.

"So how did you get your limp?"

"I got trapped. Before you came, King Next Year used to set traps all over the place."

Hearing of the little mouse's escape from death sends a shiver down Bear Cat's spine. He worries that if he cannot guard against the mice, the King will likely use the traps again! This little mouse's life, and Floral Bitty's too, would be in great danger! Bear Cat knows

these iron traps. He trembles when recalling knife-sharp serrated blades. They are truly guillotines!

Bear Cat suddenly sinks into deep thought.

Watching him intently, Tom Thumb notices how the cat's mind begins to wander. He knows he could surely escape if he were to run away at this moment. However, he decides that running is not what he wants to do.

It even occurs to him to reach out and touch Bear Cat's hand to rouse him, but he thinks twice.

"You mice should stop nosing around and tearing up stuff in the house!" Bear Cat finally snaps back to reality and speaks to the little mouse in a solemn voice.

"But we're so hungry!" Tom Thumb blinks his anxious eyes. "There aren't any more worms and insects around."

Bear Cat smacks his teeth.

"Let me see what I can do about that."

He gives the mouse's little head a consoling pat, showing him warmth not typical of cats.

"Run along now. Later tonight, let's meet at the back wall of the house!"

*Q*ueen Last Year doesn't witness this peculiar scene. As mentioned before, she pokes her head out the window every day just once at 9 am and then heads out to the market with her basket. When she gets home, she makes friends with the kitchen until completely satisfied with her lunch preparations for the King and their little princess.

Imagine her astonishment if she had seen Bear Cat, not only not catch the mouse, but actually sit out on the balcony and whisper to him as if to a soul mate all afternoon.

Queen Last Year has neither love nor hate for Bear Cat. She just frets because Princess Ivy's cat is not living up to her expectations. She had been so eagerly hopeful, awaiting a cat with great hunting abilities. But her heart is now only full of disappointment.

"*Last year* we did have a much better cat!"

This statement of Queen Last Year's dissatisfaction is as far as her complaining goes. And deep down, it's really more of a lament than a criticism. Such a kind-hearted woman she is!

On the contrary, King Next Year is much more unrelenting.

"Perhaps I couldn't wait till *next year*."

"What do you mean, Dad?"

Princess Ivy asks with bated breath as she looks up at the King, her heart tightening in her chest.

The King doesn't look at the princess, perhaps not wanting his daughter's pleading eyes to sway his determination.

"Bear Cat has one more month to disband the mice, dear."

"What do you mean one more month, Dad?" Princess Ivy is almost moaning. "After that you're going to give him away?"

"Yes, I'll give him away. If we can't exchange him to get our old Tabby Cat back, I'll buy those iron traps again."

Hoping to change the King's mind, Princess Ivy reminds him.

"Didn't you injure your hand on those traps?"

"I would rather have an injured hand than see those mischievous mice every day."

The King responds as someone ready to martyr themselves. And the way he chews his moustache while speaking to show he means business makes Princess Ivy even more desperate.

Bear Cat doesn't know his fate has been set. At the moment, he's stretched out on the balcony, watching an oriole who has flown in from somewhere to sit and sing joyfully on a branch of the frangipani tree.

The bird is saffron-colored except for the black top of her head and her two black wings. One might imagine her having fallen into an inkwell. At least that's how the author imagines it. In Bear Cat's mind, the bird looks like a celebrity singer. And when she raises her voice in song, he believes she truly is one.

At first, Bear Cat is satisfied to half-close his eyes and listen. But just moments later, a different desire begins to bubble up in his heart: he wants to catch the bird. He doesn't understand such a desire. Mice he can ignore, but it's somehow different when it comes to birds. Watching the oriole sing with her head slightly tilted and looking around seems to trigger his hunting instinct out of nowhere. The bird-catching desire becomes so robust that he can feel his body burn with anticipation.

Unfortunately, the bird is out of his leaping distance. Among the many branches of the neighbor's frangipani tree, some that stretch all the way over to the palace balcony where Bear Cat lies, the oriole sits on the one furthest away, beside the air conditioning unit, perhaps enjoying its warmth.

From time to time, the bird flits between branches, but never comes close enough to the cat.

Bear Cat attempts to climb the branches, softly sneaking through the leaves to approach her.

He notices the bird looking back at him, but her expression of indifference and the way she simply turns her head back without the slightest air of worry drives him mad.

However, just before Bear Cat can launch himself at her, the clever bird flaps off into the sky.

*B*ear Cat quickly forgets the bird.

However, he doesn't forget Floral Top—not in the slightest. But just as he's about to sink into the depths of his longing, he suddenly remembers the mice and their upcoming meeting that evening. So, he plops down to think.

Meanwhile, Tom Thumb is also thinking about Bear Cat.

When Tom Thumb returns to his cave, the entire mice commune gathers around him to carry him in triumph like a hero returning from war.

"Attaboy, Tom Thumb!" A lady mouse's tender voice is accompanied by an adoring gaze.

"In all my days, never have I seen a mouse dare to toy with a cat like that!" An old grandpa mouse applauds.

"And what's more, he hasn't got a scratch on him!" An old grandma mouse proudly continues.

It goes without saying that his peers are absolutely ecstatic. In a boisterous mass, they rush at him from all sides—someone pulling his right ear, someone pulling his left, someone pulling his tail, others tugging at his whiskers.

The whole gang excitedly fights over anything protruding from his body that they can grab.

"Why didn't Bear Cat dare do anything to you, Tom Thumb?"

"Did he know you know martial arts?"

"Did he beg you to spare him and stop messing with him?"

"I was watching from a crack in the door and saw everything with my own eyes! The cat was crying and begging for his life!"

Tom Thumb is practically crushed under the pile of questions. He stretches his head above the others to babble some reply.

"No, not at all! Not that at all!" But of course, not one mouse cares to listen.

It takes about an hour for our hero to escape the burden of victory. He immediately heads out to find Mademoiselle Guinea Pig.

Once they're a safe distance from the crowd, the two cuddle up next to each other in a hidden corner of the dark cave.

Floral Bitty doesn't ask any questions or offer any praise for Tom Thumb. She simply shows him a grain of corn and whispers: "Go ahead and eat. I saved it for you!"

Tom Thumb doesn't open his mouth to speak either. Feeling touched, he quietly munches on the grain. He suddenly remembers Bear Cat's word of "girlfriend". He mutters to himself in a state of bewilderment.

"So is that what a girlfriend is? Someone who plants a tenderness in your heart whenever you're beside them?"

24

If there's anyone in the mice commune irritated by Tom Thumb's safe return, it's Professor Grande Sewer Rat.

"The little imp not only survived, he became a hero!" Prof. mutters to himself in bitter resentment. This knife-like thought pierces his brain and gives him a massive headache.

However, Professor Grande Sewer Rat can't find any reason to punish Tom Thumb further. The little mouse carried out all his commands in earnest.

When Tom Thumb announces that he has an important meeting with Bear Cat to settle the food problem and advises the other mice to stop breaking into the palace to pillage the grain sacks, the rageful

Professor Grande Sewer Rat can't decide how to handle Tom Thumb.

These days, famine is spreading like an epidemic. Worms and insects are becoming scarce. Queen Last Year has replaced most of the paper sacks in the palace with metal barrels. The mice must now pick through trash heaps on the streets in search of food. And not just a few of them have become the easy prey of feral cats.

Prof. Sewer Rat is well aware of the situation: to oppose Tom Thumb now means opposing the entire mice commune.

He can only wait for Tom Thumb to fail. He doesn't believe a cat would ever care for a mouse's food. Even in his wildest dreams, he has never even imagined something like that happening.

"When he fails, then I'll be able to bring him down for good! Shaking hands with the enemy—such an offense cannot be tolerated!" Professor Grande Sewer Rat solemnly strokes his moustache as if adjusting his antenna to begin recording the mouse's every move.

That evening, Tom Thumb returns with a sack of rice.

A small sack of rice may not seem like much, but it's enough to transform the dull eyes of the mice into sparkling little stars that shine up and down excitedly in the dark cave.

One mouse asks, "From Bear Cat, eh?"

Another mouse adds, "Oh, I can't believe my eyes!"

"The cat is plotting something, perhaps?" A grandpa mouse wonders as he nibbles on a grain of rice, his head leaning over Tom Thumb so that his whiskers brush against the little mouse's flap of ear.

The young mice see life through a different lens, feeling more proud than suspicious.

"So, you ordered Bear Cat to pay tribute to you, right?"

"And from now on, his duty will be to serve us, right?"

Tom Thumb doesn't know how to respond to the questions from the young or the old.

He knows they're all thinking irrationally, but even he can't come up with a rational explanation for Bear Cat's actions.

"That's not it! Not at all!" Tom Thumb vigorously shakes his head, repeating over and again the only sentence he can say about the situation.

Before anyone can inquire into what he means by 'not at all,' Tom Thumb hobbles off in a hurry.

He knows his Mademoiselle Guinea Pig must be waiting for him somewhere in a hidden corner.

*T*he next evening, Tom Thumb returns with two sacks of rice. Floral Bitty had to go along with him this time to lend a hand.

Bear Cat had poured his whole serving of food into a nylon bag and hidden it behind a cardboard box next to the pink rain lilies at the edge of the balcony.

The cardboard box is Bear Cat's sleeping spot. On clear days, he likes to curl himself up in the box so that he can still poke his head out to admire the floating clouds and sparkling night stars while breathing in the fresh air. On rainy days, Princess Ivy prepares a canvas roof to protect him from the rain.

After hiding his sacks of rice behind the cardboard box, Bear Cat runs into the house for Princess Ivy. He incessantly purrs while scratching her sleeve.

At first, the Princess doesn't understand what he wants. Only when she sees the clean dish on the balcony does she realize the reason for all his meowing—he must be hungry.

"What happened today, Bear Cat? You didn't go hunting and you're still hungry?"

Princess Ivy is amazed. Though she scolds him, her voice is full of excitement. If you could only see how happy she was to take the dish back to the kitchen and prepare another serving of rice for her cat.

27

*A*nd as is typical with the flow of life (though atypical for the lives of a cat and mouse), Bear Cat and Tom Thumb soon become a pair of friends.

After delivering the sacks of rice to the mouse cave, Tom Thumb starts creeping back out to the edge of the balcony to hang out with Bear Cat at night.

Tom Thumb likes spending time with Bear Cat not just because the cat feeds his mice commune. He is also taken by Bear Cat's poetic verses.

Lying there in the night, the little mouse gets enchanted listening to the cat reciting his poems.

> *Call your name as the wind*
> *You fly up to mountains*
> *Call your name as the spring*
> *You flow down to the oceans*

Call your name as the memory
You grow more distant
Call your name as the waiting
Who knows when you will be home

So I will simply call you
Floral Top, as I wish
And every day my bliss
Comes and goes with you...

Tom Thumb loves it. With half-closed eyes, he listens and lets his soul float along with the sounds and rhythms, repeating each line in his head to learn them by heart.

"Your poems are so beautiful, brother!"

"I write them for my girlfriend, you know." Bear Cat responds, full of pride, naturally striking a familial tone with the little mouse.

"And her name is Floral Top?" The mouse begins to vaguely understand the meaning of "girlfriend".

"Yeah."

"So where does she live now?"

"She's very far away."

His voice suddenly lowers as he hesitantly tells Tom Thumb of his beloved Floral Top and the circumstances of their parting.

Word by word, every detail of the story pitter-patters down on the mouse's soul as drops of sadness.

Tom Thumb realizes that he likes the cat more and more every day.

In the evening under the stars, after parting with Bear Cat and returning to his cave, Tom Thumb lies next to Mademoiselle Guinea Pig, Floral Bitty. The little mouse finds himself melancholically humming the cat's lines in his head.

The next thing he knows, he is reciting the poem aloud, almost unconsciously.

> *Call your name as the wind*
> *You fly up to mountains*
> *Call your name as the spring*
> *You flow down to the oceans...*

Mademoiselle Guinea Pig widens her eyes.

"Oh, so beautiful! Is that your poetry?"

Tom Thumb is about to say it's Bear Cat's poem, not his, but Floral Bitty's adoring gaze makes him pause.

He gives a hesitant "Yes" and then tries to overcome his shyness to continue reciting the rest of the poem. He artfully changes one word in the last stanza.

> *So I will simply call you*
> *Floral Bitty, as I wish*
> *And every day my bliss*
> *Comes and goes with you...*

Mademoiselle Floral Bitty feels as if her soul is bathed in creamy goodness. She looks up at Tom Thumb with sparkling eyes.

"I want to hear more!"

"Tomorrow night then?"

"No, I want to hear more right now!"

Mademoiselle Guinea Pig rubs her soft warm back against Tom Thumb's, gracefully waving her beautiful whiskers. All of her movements leave the little mouse bemused and delighted. He scratches his ear, a little embarrassed.

"I haven't finished the new poem yet."

Mademoiselle Floral Bitty urges the young mouse to recite poetry for her every day. Therefore, Tom Thumb must crawl up to the balcony and plead with the cat to share more poems every day.

He listens to Bear Cat's poems, copying him until he can remember every line. Afterwards, replacing all the instances of "Floral Top" with "Floral Bitty" is as easy as pie.

So it is that every day Tom Thumb goes out to see the cat, he carries back with him a loving gift in which he can soak Mademoiselle Guinea Pig's heart.

On one of these outings, he encountered some danger. It was a rainy night and so Princess Ivy brought a flashlight out to the balcony to set up the cat's canvas roof.

Bear Cat was reciting a poem when the balcony door opened. He immediately grabbed the little mouse by his neck and hid him behind his back.

Caught off guard, Tom Thumb let out a panicked cry.

"Squeak! Squeak! Squeak!"

Princess Ivy swung the flashlight over to the cat's box, her eyes wide with surprise.

"Did you hear that squeaking, Bear?"

Bear Cat looked up at his mistress with a puzzled expression on his face, as if to say, *Perhaps your ears are playing tricks on you. I hear nothing at all!*

Princess Ivy turned round, the light in her hands sweeping the area. She stretched her ear in one direction then the other, finally confirming:

"There must be a mouse somewhere around here!"

Her voice was so determined, as if she had already seen the mouse—if not its whole body, then at least a piece of its tail. Tom Thumb, hiding behind Bear Cat's back, was frozen with fear. He squeaked uncontrollably again.

"Squeak! Squeak! Squeak!"

Once more, Princess Ivy flashed the light toward the cat's face, following the sound that seemed to apparently come from where the cat was lying.

She was surprised to see Bear Cat's mouth open as he mimicked the squeaking sounds.

"Squeak! Squeak! Squeak!"

With her eyes glued to Bear Cat's face, Princess Ivy now believed that the squeaking was coming from the mouth of the cat himself.

"Are you taking up mouse language?"

The Princess was utterly amazed. Meanwhile, Bear Cat gave the little mouse behind his back a gentle nudge, signaling for the fool to shut up.

Bear Cat worried that he wouldn't be able to keep up his lip-syncing if the little mouse continued squeaking.

"Are you sure, sweetie?"

Queen Last Year reveals her astonishment as she listens to Princess Ivy recount what she witnessed the night before.

"I'm telling the truth. I saw everything clearly with my own eyes. Our Bear Cat made these sounds: Squeak! Squeak! Squeak!"

The Queen sets her knitting down in her lap in an attempt to focus her thoughts. She furrows her brow before further wondering.

"But why would our Bear Cat need to learn mouse language? I suppose a cat can live a perfectly lovely cat life without knowing any foreign language."

"Perhaps our Bear Cat wants to use the mice's language to lure them." Princess Ivy infers, unable to think of a better explanation.

Queen Last Year, one hand rolling the ball of wool back and forth in her lap, the other excitedly waving the knitting needs, speaks—or rather, nearly elevates her voice to an exclamation.

"Yes! And that's why we haven't seen any mouse damage in our house lately!"

"I suppose Bear Cat has already caught most of them!" Princess Ivy claims, her face glowing as she recalls the King's one-month deadline.

King Next Year dismisses the news with a wave of his hand.

"I don't believe it. There are still mice everywhere."

Reacting to her husband's attitude, Queen Last Year can only widen her eyes and hum an "uhhh" sound.

"*Uhh* what!?" The King shrugs, his moustache twitching. He resembles a grumpy old mouse. "Did I say something wrong?"

"I am not sure..." Queen Last Year hesitates. "It's true, I haven't seen any sign of damage from those mischievous mice. Thinking back to *last year...*"

"A horde of mice who don't cause damage are still a horde of mice!" The King cuts in, sounding like he's quoting a philosophy textbook.

Queen Last Year is to hum another "uhh", but catches herself just in time.

"What do you mean, Dad?" Princess Ivy asks, feeling that she should speak up. The way she stares expectantly at the King reveals that she is waiting for the least bad explanation, that is, an explanation that has the least to do with Bear Cat's fate.

The King taps his fingers on the table, a gesture he reserves for getting people's attention.

"I just want to point out that the horde of mice in this house are still scampering around; they haven't gone anywhere!"

"But..." Princess Ivy almost rises from her seat, but the King stops her before she can utter another word.

"If they haven't destroyed anything recently, maybe it's because they're having tooth issues. They may not be able to chew but they can certainly squeak! Do you think I can sleep soundly with their nightly choir?"

The King exhales sharply.

"Based on their nighttime squeaking, I would guess there is not a single mouse missing from this house!"

He then delivers his final word, devastating to Princess Ivy.

"That cat is absolutely a good-for-nothing cat!"

*B*ear Cat is just as depressed as Princess Ivy.

He recalls the moment of Princess Ivy's soft embrace, the way she ran her fingers through his fur while almost whimpering.

"Poor Bear! They stopped destroying things but didn't stop their nighttime squeaking. You hear them too, don't you?"

She had looked down at him then, her beautiful hair falling over his forehead.

"Seems you haven't caught a single mouse in a while, right? But you can certainly copy their sound so well, can't you!"

Bear Cat had stayed silent in Princess Ivy's lap. Though he heard everything she said, he couldn't find the words to speak, in either the language of cats or mice.

His worries had locked both his mouth and mind shut. Bear Cat felt as if his brain had curdled and not a single idea could take root or grow.

He had tried his best to help that little mouse and his commune. He'd done everything a cat could do—and even done things other cats would never dream of doing.

But then, everything went wrong. The squeaking continued.

Mouse squeaking is no different from cat meowing or dog barking. It's as natural as the rustling of leaves or the swishing of grass in the wind. They are sounds that belong to the natural world. How could a cat possibly control the flow of life like that? No matter how much King Next Year might have wished for a sound sleep, or the poor cat himself wished to not be thrown out of the house—it was no use.

Feeling despondent and hopeless now, Bear Cat wants to stop thinking about it. He lets his mind drift like a cloud.

He soon feels his heart melting into cloud-like billows and a tender nostalgia begins to wash over him.

Has the sun risen yet where you are?
How cold must the midnight wind be?
Winter is coming, my darling afar,
Floral Top, snuggle into your coat, please!

*P*rincess Ivy is worried; Bear Cat is worried; and Tom Thumb worries too, once he hears the story.

He doesn't know how to help Bear Cat—or more precisely, help himself and his mouse commune.

If Bear Cat gets thrown out, a crueler cat will surely take his place. Or worse, iron traps with their razor sharp blades will be set everywhere.

Tom Thumb can advise the mice to stop sneaking into the palace and tearing open sacks of seeds and beans, but he can't tell them to stop squeaking at night—just like he can't tell the sun to stop rising each day.

To ease his sadness and console himself, Tom Thumb picks up a pencil and starts doodling.

He draws a mouse. He gets bored of drawing grandpa mouse, grandma mouse. So, he starts drawing Mademoiselle Guinea Pig. He draws her in every picture. Mademoiselle Guinea Pig climbing. Mademoiselle Guinea Pig walking. Mademoiselle Guinea Pig running. Mademoiselle Guinea Pig sleeping.

Then he draws himself—sleeping on a patch of green grass, under the shade of a catnip plant.

And like any sleeping mouse would be, he is dreaming in his drawing. He illustrates his dreams through a series of expanding circles. The circles fly out of his head as though he's blowing bubbles from

his ears. In the largest circle, we see his Floral Bitty peacefully sleeping, like a mango patiently waiting to ripen.

This is how the little mouse depicts a dream of his "girlfriend".

When Tom Thumb gifts the drawings to Mademoiselle Guinea Pig, she chisels a secret nook in which to hide them.

Neither of the pair want anyone else to see the drawings, afraid that they might laugh.

*A*fter drawing mice, Tom Thumb turns to drawing cats.

Before Prof. Grande Sewer Rat's orders, Tom Thumb had never drawn a cat. The one that Prof. forced him to draw was his first cat.

Prof. Sewer Rat's intention had been cruel: to send him to his death by making a provocative picture and parading it back and forth in front of the palace cat.

Ironically, Tom Thumb not only survived the ordeal, he ended up forming an unusual friendship with the cat right before the malevolent eyes of Professor.

But Tom Thumb no longer cares what Prof. Rat thinks of him—he likes Bear Cat more and more.

Bear Cat gives him food.

Bear Cat gives him poems.

And now, Bear Cat gives him the chance to draw cats by becoming his model.

Never before has Tom Thumb been able to draw such dynamic cats.

He draws Bear Cat climbing. He draws Bear Cat walking. He draws Bear Cat running. He draws Bear Cat sleeping.

He even draws Bear Cat lying beside a little mouse, undoubtedly himself.

Finally, he draws Bear Cat sleeping on the balcony, next to the fence covered in the little pink flowers of rain lilies.

And in the cat's sleep, there is a series of expanding circles.

In the largest circle, he draws a calico mademoiselle—graceful and elegant.

Bear Cat dreams of his "girlfriend"!

Tom Thumb faintly smiles as he brushes the final stroke of his drawing, believing that Bear Cat will love it very much.

35

"Ah, a bit similar!" Bear Cat comments while gazing at the drawing, his eyes full of emotion.

"Only a bit?" Tom Thumb questions, slightly pouting.

"Yeah. Floral Top's tail is longer."

Tom Thumb intently focuses on fixing the tail.

"And Floral Top's ears are smaller."

Tom Thumbs carefully adjusts the ears.

"And all the colorful spots on her body... here, and here, and here, and here..."

As Bear Cat points at the drawing, his fingers flit about the paper almost like a general directing combat officers toward their firing positions on a military map.

The little mouse-officer erases, draws again, erases once more, and redraws once again, following the cat-commander's instructions.

After a long while of diligent work on his drawing, Tom Thumb's tiny eyes look up to the cat.

"Is it identical yet, brother?"

"Yes! Very much!"

Though Bear Cat gives praise, his eyes betray a faraway look.

Tom Thumb looks inquiringly at the cat, but remains silent. He knows this cat is missing another.

And though he is still a young mouse, he can relate. His heart often aches in the absence of another.

In those moments, not even the whole blue sky is large enough to contain the sadness of those hearts.

*A*fter a while, it seems Bear Cat reaches the end of his reverie. He places his paw gently on Tom Thumb's shoulder.

"Hey, Tom Thumb!"

"Yes?"

"I need to tell you something."

"What is it, brother?"

"You've made an impressively lifelike drawing of sister Floral Top!"

"Yes?" Tom Thumb is still confused, not quite understanding what Bear Cat is getting at.

Bear Cat glances up at the sky outside and lowers his voice.

"Can you make many more drawings like that?"

"How many is 'many'?"

"I'm not sure."

Tom Thumb licks his lips, as if he's getting ready for an ice cream.

"Ten, then?"

"More!"

"Twenty?"

"Still not enough."

Tom Thumb scratches his ears in thought.

"Alright brother, one hundred?"

Bear Cat purses his lips.

"I'm not sure if even one hundred would be enough."

Tom Thumb's head spins as he tries to grasp what's going on.

"Wait, what will you do with all these drawings?"

"We'll go out and stick them on the walls of every street."

"On the walls?"

"Yeah, starting with our house."

"What for?"

"If Floral Top sees them, she'll know how to find me."

"Ah, I see. She'll follow the drawings to trace her way here."

"That's right!"

"There will need to be a lot of drawings."

"Can you do that?"

"I can do it. I want to meet Floral Top someday!"

Bear Cat's expression seems to get emotional. He sniffs.

"You will meet her."

"So, should I start drawing today?"

"Yes, today, right now."

From that day on, Bear Cat begins collecting (and sometimes stealing) every paper he can find around the palace. He brings them all to the little mouse artist.

Tom Thumb has only one task from morning until night: draw, draw, draw.

A gang of young mice gathers around to noisily discuss his work.

"Who is the cat you're drawing?"

"A calico cat?"

Tom Thumb whispers, "That's Sister Floral Top!"

"Who is Sister Floral Top?"

His voice grows mysterious, "You guys don't know her!"

"So you know her?"

"Me? I... I don't know her either."

"Hee hee hee!"

In the evenings, Tom Thumb and Floral Bitty sneak out with Bear Cat to go paste the drawings to every wall up and down the street.

The trio ventures further each night, through different quarters, reaching new streets, passing through many different neighborhoods.

They divide up to cover more ground in different directions (in truth, Bear Cat can't remember which direction leads to his old house). They fill as much wall space as possible with portraits of the calico mademoiselle.

It's not just once that Tom Thumb and Floral Bitty are threatened by street cats. But Bear Cat always manages to show up in time, returning home with wounds to prove it.

38

"What happened to you, Bear?" Princess Ivy eventually spots the scrapes on Bear Cat's body.

"You got into a fight with the mice, didn't you?"

With many patches of his fur ripped away to expose his skin, Ivy can clearly see scratches.

"So they beat you and left you like this?"

Even worse, his left ear is torn.

"But how is it possible that mice could do this kind of thing to a cat?"

With Princess Ivy being so nervous and worried, you need not be as perceptive as the author to imagine that her eyes were brimming with tears.

Bear Cat, though he can hear and understand everything going on around him, cannot speak human language.

And even if he could speak human language, he wouldn't know what to say. It would be impossible to tell her truly that he was attacked by other cats while defending mice. Only God could believe such a tale! And Princess Ivy is no saint.

"Should I leash you up so you don't get into any more fights?"

The moment she asks the question, Bear Cat immediately leaps to a high branch on the frangipani tree.

"Oh don't be scared, I'm just kidding."

Princess consoles him in a low voice. She doesn't want to tie this cat up at all. If there was a cat on earth so useless that he had to be tied up just to avoid being attacked by mice, it would be perfectly justifiable for King Next Year to throw out such a cat. No one could argue otherwise.

ℋnd just as Bear Cat received a severe beating, so too does Tom Thumb come to be beaten severely.

"That lame one!" Professor Grande Sewer Rat roars upon seeing a pile of cat drawings. His voice is like the clattering of pots and pans, so startlingly brutal.

Here might be a good place to give a bit of background on Prof. Grande Sewer Rat. He is not, in fact, a citizen of the cave. The cave here, with its network of paths beneath the soft, damp ground, is mouse country. Before Sewer Rat got lost and wound up here, the mice had plenty of food reserves stored in the cave, as was their habit.

Sewer Rat had been living in the sewers and frequenting the trash heaps beside the market to hunt for food. But there came a night when some rat-

hunters appeared. Long bamboo sticks pierced the sewer and Sewer Rat trembled to witness many of his accomplices get caught in the nets set at the sewer entrance. The long claws of sewer rats make it unlikely for them to escape a net.

Sewer Rat was lucky to fall into a crack in the pipe and escape. He ran like the dickens, scared out of his mind. It was fate that drove him to the palace, where he strayed into the territory of the mice commune.

He somehow found himself ascending to Godfather of the commune. For beside all those tiny mice, his dirty, wet, and gigantic appearance seemed mammoth. What's more, Sewer Rat was a savagely devious and ravenous rat.

After one week in the commune, he had gobbled up their entire stock of food.

With their outsized appetites, sewer rats are not generally satisfied with only cereal and insects. Even the cooked rice that Tom Thumb has been bringing home thanks to Bear Cat's help is not enough to satisfy Sewer Rat.

Every night now, he orders a group of young mice to go scrounge around the trash heaps in search of more food for him. A menacing task for mice, many have fallen into the mouths of street cats.

Though quite displeased with him, no one in the commune dares to directly confront this Sewer Rat. He threatens to call up the whole pack of sewer rats to sweep clean the cave if necessary.

And no one really knows if Sewer Rat ever had any formal education, or if he just keeps calling himself a professor. To top it all off, he grants himself permission to not lift a finger to work, but lectures others on the moral principles of being... a mouse. He even appoints himself as judge of all speech and behavior in the commune.

In the commune, it's only Tom Thumb, the tiniest of the little mice, who dares to ruffle the Prof. Grande's fur.

$\mathcal{I}$t happens thusly.

While Prof. Grande Sewer Rat lectures on the vicious cruelty of cats, Tom Thumb uses his artistry to create a tender, graceful, and in fact quite lovely mademoiselle calico.

What's more, he doesn't draw just a single portrait; he draws hundreds.

As he has done many times before, Prof. Sewer Rat grabs the little mouse by the ears and lifts him into the air. With his other hand, he taps his long stick against the scattered pile of drawings on the ground. His booming voice roars.

"What kind of trash are you drawing? Huh?"

As the little mouse begins mumbling his reply, Prof. continues to bombard him with shouting.

"Cats! Cats! Cats!"

Prof. delivers a strong kick to Tom Thumb who is suspended in the air.

"They are thorns! They are poison! They're not flowers!"

After each kick, the little mouse swings back and forth in the air, looking like a cotton pendulum.

The other mice witness the punishment in silence, their eyes full of worry and fear.

Floral Bitty timidly speaks up:

"Dear Prof...."

But before the guinea pig can finish, Prof. Sewer Rat interrupts her, his eyes blazing with malicious anger.

"You too! You and that crippled fool are in cahoots! You thought I didn't know!"

Prof. drops his stick to the ground and grabs Mademoiselle Guinea Pig by the ears.

Now, two little rodents dangle like a pair of earrings swaying in the air.

Tom Thumb so far hasn't said a word about the Prof.'s punishments. He endures them, not wanting to disrupt Bear Cat's plan. As soon as he's released, he knows he will sneak away and find the most hidden corner to make his drawings. He's determined to never let Prof. Grande Sewer Rat see him again.

Up until the moment when Prof. Grande also grabs Floral Bitty by the ears, he has been suffering in silence.

But when Mademoiselle Guinea Pig blurts out a painful moan, all of Tom Thumb's plans immediately vanish.

"Put her down!" He screams. His voice is so loud that everyone freezes, eyes wide in shock. Never before has the scream of a mouse made the cave's ceiling reverberate so powerfully.

And never before has the mouse commune witnessed a tiny mouse dare to shout back at Prof. Sewer Rat.

Prof. Rat is just as stunned. He takes three big steps back, totally flustered, and releases his grip on the little rodents who tumble to the ground.

"Run, Floral Bitty!"

Tom Thumb casts another urgent scream before turning to race away.

But Floral Bitty is not fast enough. Still paralyzed by the shock of the moment, Prof. Sewer Rat is able to swiftly grab her by the neck before she can react.

"Squeak! Squeak! Squeak!"

Floral Bitty cries out in pain, perhaps as Prof. Sewer Rat concentrates all his rage into his one forceful grip.

After hobbling a few steps forward, Tom Thumb rushes back.

The little mouse launches himself through the air at Prof. Grande Sewer Rat like a bullet, as if a spring were attached to his tail. Compared to the previous time he was launched through the air, when Prof. threw him against the cave wall, the determination in his body this time makes him much more powerful.

If shouting back at Prof. had been an earth-shattering event, attacking him is even more earth-shattering. It's something that a mouse has never had the chance to see in their entire life.

Yet here it is. Unfolding now before their eyes. And all thanks to the tiniest mouse among the little mice.

*O*f course it was the power of love, that incredible launch.

Love grants humans (and mice) a strength so extraordinary that, even if the person (or mouse) isn't yet conscious of being in love, they are still capable of doing unbelievable acts.

If mice had a Valentine's Day, perhaps the little mouse would soon realize that he is in love. As it is, he still only has a vague understanding of Bear Cat's word "girlfriend".

But perhaps love need not be fully understood. When the humans (and mice) first walked this earth and began to feel affection and then longing for each other, they most likely did not have the word "love", in either human or mouse language.

Life always precedes language; and language follows life. Language clings to life, observing everything closely. When life presents an unprecedented event, language evolves a suitable word to describe and name that event.

It's the same for little mice everywhere. They fall in love, make families, and eventually learn to say "I love you" to one another.

The most significant thing in love isn't understanding it, but sensing it. It is through the senses—not through analysis of the senses—that things transform into love.

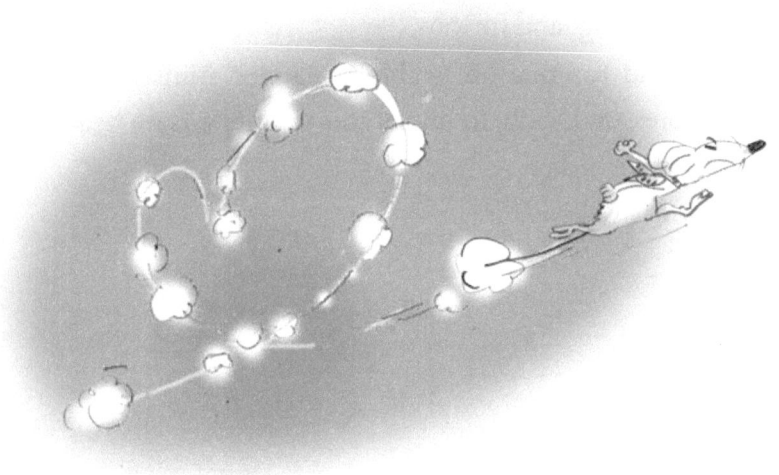

Tom Thumb was unaware of his love for Mademoiselle Guinea Pig. Yet he did sense the tenderness of lying beside her. He felt a breathtaking happiness when she shyly offered him a grain of corn. And he felt pride when whispering into her ears the stolen verses of Bear Cat's love poetry:

> *How cold must the midnight wind be?*
> *Winter is coming, my darling afar,*
> *Floral Bitty, snuggle into your coat, please!*

Now, to hear Mademoiselle Guinea Pig crying in fear, Tom Thumb completely forgets that he is just a little house mouse.

A furnace ignites in his heart—burning, gut-wrenching, and furious.

And for this he is able to launch himself at the Professor. Death, to him at this moment, is no heavier than a whisker.

This is love.

*L*ike every other rodent in the cave, Prof. Grande Sewer Rat never imagined Tom Thumb would dare attack him.

Shouting back was enough, already beyond what the Professor could fathom. But attacking him? That was utterly impossible. For how could a little mouse conceivably attack a giant sewer rat? Even with plenty of courage and a martyr's spirit, a little mouse would simply never physically measure up to a giant sewer rat.

Prof. Grande Sewer Rat could never in his wildest dreams have imagined that Tom Thumb would fire his body at him like a bullet.

Though the bullet couldn't pierce through his body, it was powerful enough to make him fall down—partly from his lack of vigilance, and partly from the mouse's incredible force.

The mice in the cave take immense pleasure in watching Prof. fall to his back on the wet ground. However, they dare not cheer. There are only a few stifled giggles from the younger mice who cannot contain their emotion.

It's fortunate for those little ones that Prof. Grande Sewer Rat is too consumed in rage to mind their squeaking giggles.

His mind boils with fury, like a pressure cooker on the verge of explosion. All he can think about is grabbing Tom Thumb by the neck and grinding his body into thousands of pieces.

After knocking Prof. to the ground with his charge, Tom Thumb also collapses, his mind dizzy from the severe impact. However, he manages to quickly rise and scramble toward a small recess in the cave, not waiting for Prof. Rat to regain his bearings.

Floral Bitty is less stunned this time than before. She pauses only for a second before dashing off in a different direction. But because Floral Bitty starts running slightly after Tom Thumb, Prof. Rat is closer to the guinea pig than the little mouse.

Though, as mentioned before, Prof. Sewer Rat is not interested in anyone else besides Tom Thumb at

that moment. After picking himself up, he immediately launches himself into a full sprint after the little mouse. With his whiskers bristling, his fur standing on end, Prof. looked almost insane.

And thus even more terrifying!

44

The scene truly resembles a ceremonial procession.

Tom Thumb leads the way, with Prof. Grande Sewer Rat close behind. Following Prof. is a band of little mice, their hearts burning with both curiosity and fear. And Mademoiselle Guinea Pig now brings up the rear, joining the crowd of bobbing tails.

The little mice chase after, unsure of exactly what they'll do, but convinced that they'll act if Tom Thumb finds himself in danger. They can't yet imagine what that action might be, but they know it will be something monumental—something they've never done before.

Tom Thumb turns left, then right, running as fast as his legs can carry him. His heart tightens as he hears Prof.'s heavy breath draw closer, inching up to his tail.

He knows he can't outrun him, no matter how strong his legs are, not to mention his limp.

The distance between him and the Prof.—rhetorically speaking, the distance between life and death—narrows with each passing second. Tom Thumb can almost measure it in the angry hiss of Prof. Rat's breath, which grows closer with every stride.

If it weren't for all the winding paths of the cave, Prof. Sewer Rat would have caught Tom Thumb by now. And just as the little mouse feels the sharp claws of the sewer rat clamping down on his head, another turn opens up before his eyes.

The chase is becoming increasingly unequal, like a race between an airplane and a car, with the poor car having a flat tire.

The twists and turns of the cave can delay the inevitable, but they can't change the mouse's fate.

The faster Tom Thumb runs, the weaker he feels. His legs refuse to obey his mind any longer.

Just when he is totally out of breath and on the verge of collapse, as he is ready to let go and surrender to whatever fate awaits him, a shining spot of light appears ahead.

45

The small bright spot cast upon the ground resembles a tiny coin made of pure light.

And indeed, it is light. Sunlight filters through the little hole of an air vent in the narrowest part of the cave, creating a shining dot.

The "light at the end of the tunnel" here appears to be literally and metaphorically true.

Without a second thought, and with no time to hesitate, Tom Thumb takes a deep breath, gathers every last ounce of his strength, and then scurries up the cave wall to dive into the hole.

"Haha! Caught you, sonny!"

Prof. Grande Sewer Rat erupts into malicious laughter. He crawls up to the hole so quickly that he almost catches Tom Thumb's tail with his teeth.

At this point, the curtain is nearly drawn. All eyes of the mice community anxiously watch from the floor, whispering among themselves.

Mademoiselle Guinea Pig gazes at the little hole, which is no longer radiating a hopeful light but instead appears gloomy and foreboding. She tilts her white ear and tilts her black ear, but hears nothing.

She eventually retreats to a quiet corner, her eyes still glued to the cave's ceiling. The next moment, she feels her eyes welling up with tears.

Floral Bitty doesn't even dare raise her hand to wipe away her tears, afraid of being seen by the other mice.

But she can't help herself—she blurts out a pained cry.

"Oh dear... oh dear..."

46

*T*om Thumb had run and run, had crawled and crawled.

He had run when there was a clear path before him, and crawled when the cave walls narrowed to just barely let him squeeze through.

As with his back and belly rubbing against the walls, he had lost clumps of fur and skinned his body in several places.

But Tom Thumb would only feel the burning pain much later. While he was running and crawling, he felt nothing.

He had run and crawled, crawled and run, then kept crawling, always toward life. In those most urgent moments, he didn't have time to listen to his heart, to

know if it continued to beat or not. He only felt the tight strangling of his chest.

He had run so much that even now, upon leaving the tunnel and encountering the blinding flood of light and tickling shock of wind, the little mouse's legs kept on running just out of inertia.

He plunged himself forward, still full of fear, until his head banged into something solid. He recognized it as a wall of the palace.

His eyes raced up the wall to see the blue trumpet vine. And only when spotting the familiar balcony, he knew he had escaped death.

On the balcony, he could see Bear Cat, sprawled out lazily, idly casting his gaze out to the clouds.

$\mathcal{B}$ear Cat's soaring gaze drops to the spot where he's just heard Tom Thumb make a noise. He raises his body, ears alert.

A cat with old cuts and scrapes now faces a little mouse with new cuts and scrapes.

"Did you just get into a battle, little bro?" Bear Cat asks with surprise as he approaches his little friend.

"That old Sewer Rat chased me." Tom Thumb answers while panting, still bone-tired.

Bear Cat had heard about Prof. Grande Sewer Rat from Tom Thumb before.

"So where is he now?" Bear Cat grinds his teeth as he surveys the surroundings.

"I don't know. I just ran as fast as I could and didn't look back!"

The little mouse puts his hands on his chest, as if to slow his heartbeat.

"I'll get even with him one day."

Bear Cat places a paw on Tom Thumb's head and says, "You can stay here with me, brother."

"Thanks, but I should go back."

"You aren't scared the old guy will catch you?"

"I am scared. But I'm more scared that Floral Bitty will worry about me."

Bear Cat immediately thinks of his calico Floral Top. He looks at Tom Thumb with worried eyes.

"Or let me accompany you. Just in case Sewer Rat..."

Tom Thumb is touched. He understands the kindness of the cat.

"Thank you, brother." The little mouse pauses before continuing. "But the cave is so narrow, you wouldn't be able to go through..."

Tom Thumb doesn't leave right away. His heart is still drumming somewhere up in his throat, and the cruel image of Prof. Sewer Rat is like a red-hot iron rod piercing his brain, anchoring him beside the cat for a bit longer.

It was not until he had counted the thirty-sixth leaf, dropped by the neighbor's frangipani tree, that the little mouse finally recovered his senses.

Bear Cat sees him off a bit further to the mouth of the cave dug into a corner of the yard, then slowly walks back.

Tom Thumb could very well lose his life by going back, but at least he knows he's going back to his Mademoiselle Guinea Pig. And if he must die, he knows for whom and for what he dies. But though I am still very much alive, I can't do anything for my Floral Top, not even return to her.

Bear Cat forlornly tugs at one of his whiskers, feeling overwhelmed with worry and sadness.

*T*om Thumb furtively creeps back into the cave where he's liable to fall into Prof. Sewer Rat's claws at any moment.

But his strongest desire at this point is to let Floral Bitty know he's still alive after that life-threatening escape through the hole.

He wants his "girlfriend" to know that he escaped the pincers of fate, even though those pincers may snap again at any moment if he has the misfortune of meeting Prof. Grande Sewer Rat.

But nothing happens the way he imagines it.

The little mouse is welcomed right at the cave's entrance by a noisy bunch of mice.

The grandpa and grandma mice all scramble toward him, just like they would toward a juicy apple, to lift him on their shoulders. They have tears in their eyes when speaking to him.

"You made it after all, didn't you son?!"

"I thought the old Sewer Rat would have torn you to pieces!"

The lady mouse for whom Tom Thumb had drawn a beautiful portrait, with a flower basket in her hands and a bow on her head, comes over to squeeze him in an embrace. Her tears drop on his head while she sobs, "Hihh, huuu...Hihh, huuu..."

Once Tom Thumb can extract his head from her squeeze to get some air, he looks around anxiously.

"So the Professor..."

"You mean that old villain?!" An old grandpa snarls.

The little mouse is surprised.

"So..."

"He hasn't returned. But if he does, we won't leave him in peace. We've had enough of his tight grip on us."

The lady mouse has stopped crying now and gives Tom Thumb's head a pat. She echoes the grandpa mouse's forceful words.

"Grandpa here is right! Wanting to harm such a lovely little boy with a disability like you—he has certainly lost all his hu-mouse-ity!"

Grandpa mouse had spoken valiant and determined words. Lady mouse had spoken judicious and thoughtful words. But Tom Thumb couldn't listen to them any further.

A group of young mice hold hands to form a circle around Tom Thumb, shouting with all their might, much to the bemusement of Tom Thumb.

> *So I will simply call you*
> *Tom Thumb, as I wish*
> *And every day is bliss*
> *To see you trotting around...*

Tom Thumb feels his cheeks flush. He grabs the paw of the little mouse nearest to him and stammers.

"Oh..."

"Oh what?" His friend feigns confusion.

"Why... how..." Tom Thumb feels a dry burning in his throat. "How... do you know that song? Actually it's not a song."

"Of course, it's a poem. We set the lyrics to music. And made a few changes."

"But how do you..."

"Listen, Tom Thumb! Do you think if a little mouse whispers poetry to someone in a quiet cave, there's not going to be another mouse in the whole commune who hears it?"

Mademoiselle Guinea Pig doesn't appear at Tom Thumb's homecoming celebration.

She is too shy.

She had heard the little mice humming the song they made out of Tom Thumb's poem and doesn't want to become an easy target for teasing.

But actually, Floral Bitty doesn't think appearing at Tom Thumb's celebration matters that much.

What matters is that Tom Thumb being still alive on this earth, and that he will soon come back to her.

She snuggles into a dark corner, letting her heart be invaded by countless emotions. She envisions her heart as a balloon about to burst, and tears begin to sparkle on her face.

Tom Thumb crawls in just as Mademoiselle Guinea Pig's tears soak her whiskers. He silently lies down beside his girlfriend, gently touching her soft fur.

That touch, so tender, is as if to say, "I'm here now."

Mademoiselle Guinea Pig responds to that gentle touch with an equally gentle nudge, as if to say, "Yes, I know! Welcome home!"

Perhaps they both wished to say more than their touches and nudges in that moment. But after such a momentous event, it seems no amount of words would have been enough.

As is often the case, silence can speak more than words.

King Next Year glances at the calendar on the wall while stroking his chin then clears his throat in king-like fashion.

"Only ten days to go!"

"And then what, Dad?" Princess Ivy looks up at her father apprehensively, already knowing his answer.

"You ask then what?" The King claps his hands. "So this is how it will go: if the mice keep squeaking day and night, Bear Cat leaves!"

He shrugs and the princess can't tell if he is serious or not.

"He has to learn how to be a cat if he wants to come back to our house *next year*."

Princess Ivy feels something close to loss. She ponders how she could save the cat, but she can't

come up with any convincing ideas. When she finally speaks up, she hears how miserably feeble her own voice sounds.

"I think Bear Cat has been really trying, Dad. He even took up mouse language."

The King stands. He leans down on the armrest of the rattan sofa, which crackles under the weight of his majestic body.

"I need a cat who can catch a mouse! Not a cat who can speak some foreign language!"

The King's tone seems to put a period at the end of the conversation regarding Bear Cat's fate.

Queen Last Year, sitting beside them, looks despondently back and forth between the father and daughter.

Though she is not thrilled either about such a useless cat, she loves their princess and can't bear to sadden her. However, she has no idea about how to remedy the situation.

Only when the King is about to step out of the room can she force herself to open some words.

"*Last year...*"

The Queen is only capable of uttering her two favorite words out of habit. After that, a miserable look comes over her face as her mind races to come up with something else.

The desperate Queen Last Year suddenly realizes that all she can think about is that she forgot to put the baking trays in the oven.

And of course, after hesitating for a bit, her mind is finally able to let go of the kitchen and grasp an argument in defense of the cat. But by that time, the King is already out the door.

51

$\mathcal{P}$rincess Ivy starts spending more time beside Bear Cat.

She takes a rattan chair out to the balcony to read in the morning. Or she brings her embroidery exercises out there in the afternoon.

It is how she prepares for her cat's upcoming departure.

She lets out an occasional whimper whenever she pricks herself with the needle, as she cannot avoid melancholically watching her cat while embroidering.

She has this persistent feeling that she's embroidering her sadness onto the white pieces of cloth. With every stitch, the sadness appears to grow thicker and darker, which she feels poignantly.

The cat curls up at her feet, soft and helpless.

Like the Princess, Bear Cat knows that his departure date is just around the corner. The word "farewell" has been piercing his heart and making him ache for days now. For a cat's life, too, contains much sadness and joy. When sadness erupts, it can be like an embroidery needle passing through his heart.

He's thought of everything he could possibly think of, he's done everything he could possibly do to help the mice. But he simply cannot extinguish their squeaking. For who could extinguish the sound of the wind on the prairie?

Burrowed in his thoughts, he silently counts the dawns and dusks. As he counts, how he longs for Floral Top to be able to find him before he leaves the palace for somewhere else unknown.

Just ten more sunrises and ten more sunsets. Then Bear Cat will know if he will meet Floral Top again in this life or not.

> *Will be sad as a leaf*
> *Will be sad as a tree*
> *The day you come back*
> *And no longer see me...*

$\mathcal{T}$he Old Sewer Rat has still not yet come back to the cave.

Perhaps he went back to his old dirty sewers, perhaps recognizing them as his true home. At least this is what the young mice assume before they quickly forget the Old Sewer Rat and soak themselves in the festive air of freedom.

What a joy it is when someone's boot is finally lifted from your neck.

And life goes on: the little mice jump about, play tag, climb up walls, quarrel amongst themselves, and shout loudly as if every day were the Tết holidays. While the grandpa and grandma mice lean back and watch the little ones play, quietly enjoying life immersed in comfort and relaxation.

Only Tom Thumb knows that the peaceful days will be over soon.

For whenever the kind-hearted cat leaves the palace, the mice will have to return to their difficult and dangerous days of foraging.

But no matter how troubling life may be, you cannot stop it by worrying about it.

You must keep going, the little mouse thinks to himself as he takes out his papers to make more drawings of the calico cat.

Until Floral Top can find her way to the palace, he feels his debt to Bear Cat is not yet settled.

Like someone resigned to their fate, Bear Cat spends an entire afternoon emptying his mind. He bathes himself in sunlight and wind, feeling the warm air tickling his skin and seeping into his thick fur. He thinks of absolutely nothing. Ah, except for the part of the afternoon he spent composing a few verses:

> *Days become months*
> *Months become years*
> *You'll come to know*
> *The flickering is finished*
> *By the sight of its shadow*
> *Totally diminished.*

Finishing some lines, Bear Cat feels so sad that he has to plop down and let his mind float.

The oriole from the other day flies back and sits on the frangipani tree, twittering above his head.

At first, Bear Cat doesn't pay any attention to her. The bird's song simply falls into the vast emptiness of his heart then fades away just as the sounds of the afternoon wind.

But suddenly, for some inexplicable reason, his ears seem flooded with birdsong and it's the only thing he can hear.

Bear Cat looks up. The saffron-colored bird is perched nearly right above his head. Where does this boldness come from? Is it her passion for singing that makes her blind to him, or does she simply consider him nothing? *Oh perhaps I really am nothing. As lifeless as an old mop.* As Bear Cat thinks, he feels his body grow hot, both from his sudden anger and something like the pleasure of an instinct.

As if injected with a poison, the desire to pounce on that bird enters his body so powerfully that he feels his heart tighten and his legs tremble.

Before he knows it, his body is flying through the air like an arrow.

This time, the bird doesn't have a chance to flap her wings. She tries to hop away but is too late.

The cat's sharp claws catch one of the bird's wings, pulling some feathers out to send them scattering in the air, shimmering in the sunlight.

The bird jumps off the branch, trying to flap her one remaining wing. But this thrashing only serves to slow its fall.

And the bird keeps falling down.

54

$\mathcal{B}$ear Cat also falls almost immediately to the brickyard below.

But before he can get the bird in his claws, a little mouse screams from a nook in the corner of the wall.

"Don't, brother!"

Out pokes Tom Thumb's head. Peeking out from behind his head are two ears, one white one black, of Mademoiselle Guinea Pig. They both run toward the wounded bird.

Bear Cat is surprised. He stops and looks at the mice with eyes full of questions.

"Let us have the bird, brother!" Tom Thumb says, as if to explain.

"For a good meal, eh?"

The cat's question makes the bird tremble in fear. She frantically beats her wings while still laid up on the ground, looking both perplexed and desperate.

"No, not at all."

"To be friends then?" Bear Cat asks again, this time in jest.

But the little mouse unexpectedly nods his head.

"Yes."

"We are friends. We are friends." The bird suddenly speaks up. Bear Cat notices the force of her flapping subside.

For the first time in his life, Bear Cat hears the bird's voice. Her voice is not so clear, perhaps because she is used to singing.

Bear Cat sinks into another contemplation. It then dawns on him that Tom Thumb's idea is totally reasonable. If a cat can make friends with a mouse, why couldn't a mouse make friends with a bird?

He watches Tom Thumb and Floral Bitty carry the oriole to the corner of the wall.

Bear Cat is left standing there, wearing a pensive look. If it weren't for his tail gently swaying and his eyes rising to see the stars beginning to sparkle in the darkening sky, one might imagine that he himself was melting into the quiet afternoon shadow.

When night throws it blanket
Of quiet afternoon shadow
Sky whispers: Never fear
I will turn on the stars!

*B*ear Cat wanders back to his familiar spot.

The sight of the inseparable Tom Thumb and Floral Bitty fills him with unreasonably jealousy.

Once again, he thinks of his calico mademoiselle. How long has it been since they were last together? He can't remember exactly, but it feels like ages. The neighbor's frangipani tree has dropped its leaves so many times already!

As the sky shifts into night, he lies down.

A few verses stir in his mind.

It's as if someone had struck a match to his memory, rekindling the buried sadness in his heart. The unfinished poem feels like a candle, crying out to keep burning.

When our hands do part
After days side by side
The river whispers: Never fear
I will wait for you here.

When the tears do fall
After such heavy sorrow
The oriole sings: Never fear
I will gather the sparkling beads on lovely cheeks
and sew them into a fairy tale.

He recalls the oriole from this afternoon. The bird had entered his poem so naturally, as if to sooth his pain and bandage his heart's wound.

Ah, and as for wounds, he wonders, will the little mice tend to the oriole's wound tonight?

56

Three days pass.

In these last three days, King Next Year has remained indifferent when discussing the cat's departure. He gazes at the calendar's dwindling pages with something resembling triumph, while Princess Ivy's heart breaks as she watches the smug determination on his face. Queen Last Year continues her quiet sighing, her head swiveling between the King and the Princess, unsure of how to mend the growing rift between father and daughter.

On the balcony, Bear Cat sticks to his nightly task of delivering sacks of rice to the mice. He also remains lost in his melancholy rumination about the impending separation.

On the fourth day, the palace falls into an eerie silence. Not a single mouse squeak breaks the stillness.

But that doesn't mean everyone is able to sleep soundly.

Out of nowhere, a crow's rattling caws pierce the air, drilling into everyone's ears like saw blades cutting through bamboo.

The crows persist all night long. No one can manage even a wink of sleep thanks to their relentless, menacing, and mind-numbing calls.

Beyond irritated, King Next Year leaps out of bed and grabs a flashlight. He scans the trees while hissing incessantly to scare the crows away.

The fifth day is no different. As evening falls, the crows return. And they stay, cawing through the long night once again.

By morning, the King's face looks as pale and haggard as if he's been seriously illness.

"What is this? A harbinger of the apocalypse?" His voice is hoarse as he looks at Queen Last Year and Princess Ivy with tired, bloodshot eyes.

"It's the crows, dad!" Princess Ivy exclaims.

"I know it's the crows!" The King lets out a weary sigh. "But where are they?"

Queen Last Year adds her two cents, more to appease the King rather than offer any real explanation.

"Oh yes, I remember *last year* nothing odd like this ever happened."

But there is only one in the palace who knows where they are: Bear Cat.

57

That evening, when Bear Cat hands over his sacks of rice to Tom Thumb and Floral Bitty, he demands answers.

"What the hell have you guys been up to these past two days?"

"What? Nothing!"

Bear Cat snorts.

"Imitating crows—don't tell me that is not something?"

"Crows, eh?" The little mouse looks confused. "We were trying to sing like the oriole, brother!"

Bear Cat's heart sinks. He'd intended to scold the little mouse, since even he couldn't stand the cawing that grated against his ears. But the candid response from Tom Thumb touches him deeply. He realizes now why the little mouse wanted to save the bird: so the palace mice could imitate bird songs instead of squeaking. So that Bear Cat could stay with him and the mice commune.

Bear Cat nudges little mouse's rib.

"Crow-cawing is even more annoying to the ears than mouse-squeaking!"

"Is that so?"

"Mmhmm."

And so, that night, the cawing stops.

For the first time ever, King Next Year is able to sleep soundly with the squeaks of mice under his bed.

But even after waking up refreshed, the King doesn't forget to glance at the calendar before breakfast.

"Just three more days!"

58

The oriole flies away. Perhaps when Tom Thumb passed along the feedback that they sounded like crows, it killed her inspiration to teach them more. As the little mouse recounts this to the cat, he hears the cat sigh.

"We cannot fight fate, dear brother!"

The little mouse is about to reply but then decides to keep his mouth shut. He doesn't know whether he wants to console himself or the cat.

In his silence, he hears the cat murmuring.

When our hands do part
After days side by side

It makes the little mouse feel sentimental.

"Is that a new poem of yours?"

"Mmhmm."

"So sad, brother."

"Mmhmm."

"I'll be so sad when you leave."

Bear Cat pats Tom Thumb's head, a habit that accompanies his emotional state. He casts his eyes up to the sky, his voice soft.

The river whispers: Never fear
I will wait for you here.

"What does that mean?" The mouse wonders.

"It means I'll be back one day."

"Do you believe that?"

"I do."

The little mouse gets excited and moves closer to the cat, his voice full of joy.

"So do you know when you'll be back?"

"I don't know yet." Bear Cat notices the little mouse's face fall, disappointed. After a pause, apparently infected by the language of the King. "Perhaps *next year...*"

59

By the eighth day, the mice still squeak from hidden nooks and crannies throughout the night.

Bear Cat curls up helplessly on the balcony, listlessly counting fallen stars.

In the palace, on his soft bed with sheets the color of red wine, King Next Year tosses and turns, restless.

He had slept well the night before because the cries of crows had finally stopped. But after the crows leave, he finds himself tormented again by the squeaking mice.

Sullenly, he counts on his fingers, unable to see the calendar in the dark.

Princess Ivy has stopped begging and pleading with him each time he shouts the countdown. It's not from a lack of desire, but a lack of energy.

Now, she spends her time and energy sitting beside Bear Cat, caressing him more and feeding him much more. She doesn't realize that she's inadvertently helping the mice in the palace.

To see the way she cares for Bear Cat, one might think he was a very sick cat.

And Bear Cat does seem to be getting sick for real. He buries his head glumly in his little mistress's hands, his thin lips releasing a moan from time to time.

In just a few days, Bear Cat will leave the palace with no chance to see his Floral Top again.

He doesn't know if his calico mademoiselle will ever actually see the drawings pasted up around the streets. But suppose, on some beautiful day, she does happen to see one and will be able to find her way to the King's palace—and he is no longer there.

Will be sad as a leaf
Will be sad as a tree
The day you come back
And no longer see me...

*B*ear Cat can no longer sleep at night.

He lies on the floral-tiled floor, spiritless and unmoving, like a stranded ship. Thoughts about the future have been draining the life out of him.

Tomorrow will be the tenth day.

Life has not changed in the past ten days. The wind still whistles, the dewdrops still drip, the mice still squeak. And Mademoiselle Floral Top is still out there, so far away.

Recently, when delivering the sacks of rice to Tom Thumb, Bear Cat had the feeling that he was handing over a farewell gift to the mice. The idea made his load as heavy as a lead chain around the neck.

In contrast, Tom Thumb and Floral Bitty did not seem unhappy in the least. Bear Cat had wanted to ask if the oriole had ever returned, or the old Sewer Rat, but the bright freshness on their faces made him grumpy and silent, like an anger was choking his throat.

He didn't say a word when handing them the rice. He just quietly turned back and left.

And now, recalling it all, he still feels a lump in his throat.

He lays his head down in his lap and curls himself up in sadness. His plan is to lie still like this, as quiet as a wooden cat, until the next morning when he receives the King's verdict.

But something pricks up his ears. He lifts his head from his arms, then pulls himself up from the floor.

Trembling with emotion, he turns his head and anxiously looks around.

A bird's song. A nightingale's. Yes, that's it. The songs of nightingales are weaving a curtain of melodious sound around the palace.

What talented mice they are! Bear Cat silently praises them in his head when a light in the house flickers on. Then, a door swings open. As a whirlwind, the King, the Queen, and the Princess all barrel out onto the balcony.

"Bear Cat! Did you hear something?" Princess Ivy bends down, embracing the cat, tears in her eyes.

"Oh, how long it's been since we've heard a nightingale!" The Queen turns her radiant face toward the King, her voice elated, as if recalling the early days of the courtship.

The King scours the dark trees with his eyes while his hands twirl his longest whisker above his bewildered lip.

"Why would a nightingale sing at night?"

The nightingale's song doesn't only shake up those in the palace.

Everyone in the whole neighborhood also rises at the same time.

The lights in houses flick on.

The curtains of windows are drawn.

The latches of doors rattle open.

Countless heads pop out from windows or peak out over balconies.

Bear Cat slips out of Princess' arms and sneaks away into the yard. He goes in search of Tom Thumb, whom he quickly finds under the blue trumpet vines. Tom Thumb is also searching for Bear Cat.

"Amazing, brother!" Bear Cat praises him and gives him a strong pat on the shoulder.

In the cat's excitement, his pat is a bit too strong, but Tom Thumb doesn't seem to mind. He is overjoyed.

"Does it sound like a nightingale?"

"So much! Did the oriole return to the cave?"

"Yes. Sister Oriole returned and brought a friend with her, Sister Shrike. And Sister Shrike taught us to sing."

"A shrike?"

Bear Cat's eyes are wide-open. He has heard of these pearly-grey songbirds with black masks around their eyes. They are known for their ability to imitate the songs of a hundred different birds. *Yes, they must be great teachers in this subject indeed; if they were teaching, perhaps even a stone would be able to sing.* Bear Cat chirps excitedly to himself.

"No wonder!"

He gives Tom Thumb's shoulder another pat, more gently this time.

"So Oriole flew away to invite Shrike to come teach you guys the songs?"

"Yes."

The little mouse answers happily. Before Bear Cat has a chance to say anything else, a sudden burst of twittering rings in his ears. The song is miraculously clear, melodic and cheerful, melting into the other nightingales' songs and making the whole palace seem to light up.

It's Tom Thumb who sings. He is calling for the sun to rise.

*K*ing Next Year no longer has any reason to kick Bear Cat out of the house. In a mysterious fashion that only the cat knows (and perhaps the readers of this book), the King's enemies of sleep are suddenly mute.

The mice in the palace have long since stopped nibbling on and destroying things in the palace, and now it seems they've relocated somewhere else.

In their place, the nightingales have come to roost, chirping every morning to wake the sun. Though to be honest, in the King's opinion, the birds do rise a bit too early, like an alarm clock set at the wrong time.

The King no longer looks up at the calendar every morning, and Princess Ivy feels these days to be the most beautiful and brightest of her life.

She even brings home a guitar and enthusiastically practices it while singing, as if imagining herself a nightingale.

Queen Last Year still maintains the habit of poking her head out the window to watch the cat on the balcony every day at 9 am while kneading dough. However, she no longer lets out her moody sign as before. These days, she actually looks at the cat's laziness with some admiration.

Outside in the evenings, before the nightingale orchestra starts their concert, Bear Cat usually meets up with Tom Thumb and Floral Bitty at the foot of the wall.

Tonight, Tom Thumb goes by himself to collect the rice so he and the cat linger around to talk a bit longer.

"I'm so happy that you can stay here with us." Tom Thumb gushes. Never before in his life has he felt so close to someone as he does to this cat.

But Bear Cat doesn't feel so comfortable showing so much emotion. He shares the same feeling that Tom Thumb has, that he is really happy to be able to stay in the palace. But when Tom Thumb speaks it out loud, somehow he feels a little embarrassed.

"So how about the old Sewer Rat?" Bear Cat tries to distract him by changing the topic. "You guys should be prepared in case he returns. I'll give you a hand if needed."

"Don't worry, bro! That old guy will never come back!"

"Why?"

"We just discovered that the dots of sunlight that shone through the hole have disappeared..."

"Ah, so he must have gotten stuck there? No wonder! He was such a horribly big thing!"

Bear Cat changes his voice, lowering his tone as if confiding his soul to the mouse.

"Hey, Tom Thumb!"

"What is it, brother?"

"Do you know what I'm dreaming about at the moment?"

"You must be waiting for sister Floral Top..."

And then the little mouse gasps. He sees that Bear Cat is no longer paying any attention to him.

The cat is looking up at the roof of the opposite house. His entire body trembles.

A calico cat stands on the highest point of the roof and stares down at the yard below.

Behind her, the leaves sparkle under the white moon.

Embraced in a halo of light, she looks magnificent and mysterious, as if she had just stepped out of a fairy tale.

"Is that Floral Top, brother?" The little mouse whispers, finding himself trembling with excitement as well.

"Yes, that's her..."

The cat whispers back in response.

Tom Thumb doesn't bow his head, but his voice sounds like he's praying.

"Dear heavens, she finally saw the drawings on street corners..."

"Yeah..."

With an ache in his heart, Bear Cat doesn't take his eyes off the roof for even a second. He had been waiting for this moment for so long—immersing in his lovesick memories for countless dawns and dusks, reciting countless poems. Yet upon seeing Floral Top just now, it's as if he doesn't know what to do.

He simply stands there, totally paralyzed, and looks at her with eyes red from tears.

Tom Thumb stands beside, bewilderedly looking back and forth between Bear Cat and Floral Top, not knowing if he should open his mouth.

Eventually, unable to hold his silence any longer, he gently speaks up.

"Perhaps she hasn't seen you?"

Bear Cat doesn't seem to hear any words from the little mouse. He stands rooted to his spot in the shade of the blue trumpet vines, motionless. Even his long tail shows no sign of life. Only his whiskers vibrate as the strings of a guitar.

What happened to him? The little mouse wonders. And then all of sudden, he opens his mouth widely and shouts.

"Sister Floral Top!"

64

Tom Thumb's scream spreads through the wind, loud and clear.

Bear Cat is like someone rising from a deep sleep. He blinks his eyes and his tail revives with some gentle sways.

The little mouse had pulled him out of his stupor of surprise and emotion.

But just as he's about to call his calico cat, the figure of a strange cat rises up beside her.

A big tomcat with pale yellow fur. His eyes shoot out blue rays of light.

Bear Cat isn't even able to get her lovely name past his lips; it stops and freezes there.

As if falling into an icy hole, Bear Cat's entire body startles and turns frigid.

So it's not that she didn't see him. Floral Top must have seen him from the start. But she didn't call out to him, and seemed to have no intention of meeting him.

She had followed the drawings, perhaps just out of curiosity; to know how he's living and perhaps see him for the last time.

A slight noise behind him makes Tom Thumb turn around in surprise. He sees Mademoiselle Guinea Pig crawling over and looking like she's about to ask a question. Tom Thumb hastily gestures with a finger to his mouth to signal for her to stay silent.

On the distant roof, Floral Top and the strange cat walk shoulder-to-shoulder under the moonlight, moving further and further away.

*A*fter that day, Bear Cat gets sick for almost a month. Tom Thumb goes every evening to visit him on the balcony. Once, he happens to overhear three lines of poetry.

> *What does love offer?*
> *Two cats sitting at a window*
> *One stays the other goes...*

It was a time that Bear Cat wistfully recalled when he and Floral Top sat shoulder-to-shoulder on the windowsill, watching the rain pour down on the quiet veranda on cold afternoons. As far as the author knows, these lines belong to Bear Cat's final poem.

During the time the cat was trapped in his sadness, the people of the palace and the neighborhood got

used to the nightingale's songs ushering in the early morning. Whenever the nightingales stopped, people knew a new day had begun. And everyone was happy with this odd style of alarm clock.

The story of these lovely animals now reaches its conclusion. If there's anything more to add, it would be to reveal the truth of this story's location: it is not in fact any palace of any king, as the author has repeatedly described since the beginning.

It is just a house, as normal as any other house, and not at all a palace or a castle. King Next Year is actually a truck-driver. Queen Last Year makes a living as a baker. And Princess Ivy, quite certainly, is in the 11th grade at the local high school.

The reason why the author has persisted in exaggerating such fancy images of "the King, the

Queen and the Princess" is because of this little story: the day he overheard Tom Thumb tell Mademoiselle Floral Bitty upon their first meeting, "Follow me. I will find something for you to eat." The Mademoiselle Guinea Pig had asked, "Where is your home?" and the little mouse mischievously replied, with his whiskers rising up proudly, "I live in the palace of the King."

Of course, the little mouse was showing off. But in love, sometimes showing off just adds a little flavor without harming anything. Being too honest, as Bear Cat, makes this love story end in a way the author doesn't like at all. But at the end of the day, we have to agree that it is Bear Cat's beautiful and loyal love that changes his behavior in a totally unexpected way.

Such love from a cat (or a human) radiates a sparkling light with which anyone could create some miracles in this world. Don't you think?

N. N. A.

Hồ Chí Minh City, March 7, 2012

About the Author

Nguyen Nhat Anh is a prolific, bestselling Vietnamese author who writes novels are for children and young adults with many, including the fable *Two Cats Sitting at a Window*, appealing to all ages.

After working as a teacher, the author began writing short stories, poetry, and books. Some of Nguyen Nhat Anh's notable titles include *Give Me a Ticket to Childhood*, which won the SEAsian Writers Award in 2010, *Blue Eyes, I Am Beto*, and *I See Yellow Flowers in the Green Grass*, available in English outside of Vietnam from Hannacroix Creek Books, Inc.

Anh's *Kaleidoscope series* consists of dozens of books. The author is based in Ho Chi Minh City.

www.ingramcontent.com/pod-product-compliance
Lightning Source LLC
Chambersburg PA
CBHW020332260626
47156CB00004B/1481